Starship Rescue

by

Theresa Breslin

Illustrated by Celia Chester

To Calum

First published in Great Britain by Barrington Stoke Ltd
10 Belford Terrace, Edinburgh, EH4 3DQ
Copyright © 1999 Theresa Breslin
Illustrations © Celia Chester
The moral right of the author has been asserted in
accordance with the Copyright, Designs and
Patents Act 1988
ISBN 1-902260-24-4
Printed by Polestar AUP Aberdeen Ltd

Meet the Author - Theresa Breslin

What is your favourite animal?

A small elephant with green fur

What is your favourite boy's name?

Tom

What is your favourite girl's name?

Scheherazade, the Arabian
princess, Teller of Tales

What is your favourite food?

Porridge and soup – but NOT
together!

What is your favourite music?

Bob Dylan

What is your favourite hobby?

Reading

Meet the Illustrator - Celia Chester

What is your favourite animal?

Cats

What is your favourite boy's name?

Nicholas

What is your favourite girl's name?

Chanelle

What is your favourite food?

Indian

What is your favourite music?

Classical guitar

What is your favourite hobby?

Fathoming my new P.C.!

Barrington Stoke was a famous and much-loved story-teller. He travelled from village to village carrying a lantern to light his way. He arrived as it grew dark and when the young boys and girls of the village saw the glow of his lantern, they hurried to the central meeting place. They were full of excitement and expectation, for his stories were always wonderful.

Then Barrington Stoke set down his lantern. In the flickering light the listeners were enthralled by his tales of adventure, horror and mystery. He knew exactly what they liked best and he loved telling a good story. And another. And then another. When the lantern burned low and dawn was nearly breaking, he slipped away. He was gone by morning, only to appear the next day in some other village to tell the next story.

Contents

Radio Control
Station

Merkonium
Mines

The
Fortress

Main
Gates

Main
Square

Chapter 1
Outside the Fortress

Ten seconds ... Only ten seconds.

Marc knew that was all the time he would have. Con, their leader, was very clear about that. The spy, Alex, had sent word to them from the Fortress. Tonight the Keepers would change the patrol on the main gate of the Fortress before the setting of the suns. At that time the wall just beside the gate would be safe to cross. But only for ten seconds.

1

"Ten seconds," Con repeated. "That is the length of time that the killer electric current in that section is switched off. It is to allow the guards out and in. The red warning light comes on. They are given ten seconds to change over, and then the high voltage current is switched back on again."

He put his hand on Marc's shoulder, and stared deep into his eyes.

"They tell me that you can run fast, boy. Let's hope for all our sakes that you can."

Marc looked up at Con's face. He listened carefully as he was told what he had to do. Because he was small and light, the anti-gravity belt, which he wore around his waist, would lift him up and over the wall in a few seconds. Then Marc would take the capsule with the electronic message straight to Con who would be waiting for him in the Main Square of the Fortress.

"You've studied the map?" Con asked him. "You know the way?"

Marc nodded. He knew every detail of this mission. He also knew that it was dangerous. Very dangerous.

Con then turned to the rest of the Outsiders gathered around him, deep in the caves beside the Merkonium mines.

"This is our moment," he said. "For too long Jared and the rest of the Keepers have kept us on the Outside as slaves in the mines. Tomorrow night the Starship from our home planet Earth will pass close to our world, as it does every twenty years or so. With our message capsule we will send out an SOS to them."

"If only on one of these visits they took the time to actually beam down," said one of the Outsiders bitterly. "Then they would see how we

3

are forced to slave in the Merkonium mines, while the Keepers and the Chosen Ones live in comfort within the Fortress."

"Yes," cried another. "It is time they knew how the evil Keeper Jared destroyed this planet which was once beautiful."

Con raised his hand for silence.

"It will all end soon," said Con. "Tomorrow morning I will go through the gate with my trader's pass. As you all know, the few of us who are allowed to trade in and out of the Fortress must be screened in the X-Ray booth before entering. The message capsule would be found if I carried it."

The Outsiders nodded as Con spoke.

"We have to make sure that the capsule is safely delivered to the Radio Control Station within the Fortress," said Con.

He turned and pointed at Marc.

"This boy, Marc," he told them, "will carry the message capsule across the wall to me. Then we will make our way to the Radio Control Station, place it in the transmitter, and send out our SOS ..."

All this had happened early this morning, and now, crouched in his hiding place, Marc looked at his watch. Five more minutes to wait. His hands were sweating. He wiped them along his trousers, and crouched down lower in the scrub bushes. It was the last piece of cover before the long bare stretch of ground in front of the wall. Would he manage it in time? Marc looked at the wall and tried to guess the distance he had to run.

He knew why he had been chosen. He was small enough to hide in the scrub, and light enough for his anti-gravity belt to lift him over

the wall. Any bigger or heavier and there just would not be enough time.

He had been lying all day under the heat of their planet's two suns, and now it was nearly time. The suns were low in the sky, and his watch told him that in one minute they would switch off the killer electricity beams. The red warning light would come on. Then there would be ten seconds to allow the patrol guards to enter the gatehouse and a new guard through to take their place.

Marc watched the numbers click past on his watch.

Fourteen, thirteen, twelve ... Marc got up on his knees and pulled his cloak around him.

Eleven ...

Marc's heart jumped. In the dusk the red warning light had flashed on at the gate.

It was time to run.

Chapter 2
Freedom Run

TEN!

NOW!

Marc raced towards the wall. As he ran, he counted under his breath.

Nine ... eight ... seven ... six.

Marc skidded to a halt. The high wall of the Fortress loomed above. He must switch on his anti-gravity belt.

His fingers slipped as he touched the button.

"Oh no!" he said softly.

Marc put his finger back on the button. Now he had it. He rocketed upwards.

"Four. Three ..." He counted under his breath. The smooth wall went on and on. "Two ..."

He was at the top. Marc pressed the second button to get the forward thrust. He was across the top of the wall. But he had lost a vital second or two. No time for a quiet landing. He took his finger from the button and crashed to the ground on the other side of the wall.

He rolled as he fell. Then he scrambled to his feet and limped towards some thick bushes.

As he crawled in among the branches Marc felt for the message capsule inside his jerkin. It was safe!

Then he heard voices.

"This way!"

There was the sound of running feet. Two Keeper guards were at the wall where Marc had come over.

"I'm sure I heard a noise," said one.

"Perhaps over there," said the other. He pointed directly at Marc's hiding place. "Among those bushes?"

Marc gasped in fear. The Keeper guards were walking directly towards him!

Chapter 3
Sasha

Suddenly, from behind, Marc felt a sharp tug on the hood of his cloak. A voice spoke in his ear.

"I am Sasha. Follow me."

He turned and saw a young girl with short dark hair. She was crouched down just behind him. She wore the purple cloak of the Chosen Ones.

"Hurry!" she whispered.

Then she turned and scuttled off through the trees. Keeping low, Marc ran after her. Very soon they came to the first houses of the City. All had high wooden fences round them. Sasha went up to one. She touched the surface with her hand. A section of the fence slid to one side.

She winked at Marc.

"In you go," she said.

Sasha slipped through after him and closed the panel.

"That should hold them up for a bit," she said.

She led Marc down a path and out onto the streets. Marc had never been inside the Fortress before, and he had never seen anywhere so wonderful. The gardens were full of colour.

The walls of the houses and offices were creamy pink in the light from the setting suns.

They walked for a few moments, and then the girl turned to face Marc.

"You have it with you?" she asked abruptly.

"What?" said Marc.

"The message capsule with the SOS?"

Marc felt his stomach turn over. His hands began to sweat.

"I don't know what you mean," he said.

"We don't have time to play silly games," Sasha said. "Do you carry the SOS from the Outsiders?"

Marc did not speak.

Suddenly Sasha smiled. "I know what you are thinking. *How do I know that I can trust her?*"

"Well?" said Marc. "How *do* I know I can trust you?"

She grinned at him. "You can't. Not for sure. But ..." she looked at Marc for a long moment. "I will show that I trust you. I will tell you who I am."

"You've told me who you are. You said that your name was Sasha," said Marc.

"My proper name is Alexandra," said the girl. "So I can be Sasha ... or ... Alex."

"Alex!" cried Marc. "Alex, the spy! The one inside the Fortress who sends information to the Outside?"

"Yes," said Sasha. "Everyone inside the Fortress knows me as Sasha. So, I use the name Alex when I send information to the Outsiders."

Marc waited, still unsure. "I only know you as Sasha," he said. "I still don't know if I can trust you."

"Look," said Sasha. "At this moment you can go neither forward nor back. You *have* to trust me."

Chapter 4
Inside the Fortress

"Yes," Marc said finally. "I do carry the message capsule."

"Then we must hurry," said Sasha. "Soon the streets will not be safe. Curfew time is one hour after the suns set. That is the time when everyone must be back in their own homes. Anyone still outside at that time is arrested."

She strode off down the street. Marc watched her for a moment. Then he followed her. After a few minutes he pulled Sasha into a doorway.

"This is not the way to the Main Square," said Marc.

"We are not going there," said Sasha.

"But Con said I must go to the Main Square," said Marc.

"No," said Sasha. "We will go to the Radio Control Station. We can put the message capsule in the transmitter and send it out to the Starship from Earth."

"How can we get into the Radio Control Station?" said Marc.

"I can get us both inside," said Sasha. "As long as we get there before dark."

Marc shook his head. He did not want to follow this girl any more. Con was waiting for him at the Main Square. He should go there first.

"Which is the way to the Main Square?" he asked Sasha.

"That way," pointed Sasha. "But ..."

Marc made to step out from the doorway.

She dragged him back. A patrol of Keeper guards marched past.

Sasha peered out after them. "There are more of them about than usual." She looked about her fearfully. "We must hurry to the Radio Control Station."

"No," said Marc stubbornly. "I am not going anywhere until I see Con."

Sasha turned then and stared at him.

"Don't you know?" she said. "Con has been taken."

Chapter 5
Con

"No!" cried Marc. He felt as though he had been struck.

"I'm sorry," said Sasha. "I thought you knew."

"When ..." said Marc. "When did this happen?"

"This afternoon," said Sasha.

"I have been hiding in the scrub bushes since early morning," said Marc. "I had no way of knowing that Con had been taken prisoner."

"There is talk all over the Fortress," said Sasha. "That is why I came to the wall. Jared has Con in the Truth Chamber." She took Marc's arm. "You see now why it is so important that we hurry. Soon he will tell them everything."

"He will never talk," said Marc. "Not Con."

Sasha looked at Marc, her eyes serious. "Believe me in this," she said. "Those who are taken by Jared the Keeper ..." She shuddered. "In the end, they all talk."

"We have to rescue him," Marc said firmly.

Sasha shook her head. "It is useless. Even I cannot get past those guards."

"We must at least try," said Marc.

Marc felt sick. Con was their leader. Over the last few years he had organised the Outsiders. He had stopped them bickering amongst themselves. He was the one who had thought up the plan. He had made them believe that they could get a message out to the Starship when it arrived. If he was captured then there was no hope.

"I am going to try to free him," said Marc.

"I'd *really* like to know how you intend to do that," said Sasha in a sarcastic voice. "The Truth Chamber is inside the Prison. Only Keeper guards are allowed in and out, and their passes are checked at six different electrified gates."

"I don't care," said Marc. "He has done so much for us. Now, when he needs help, I will not desert him."

Sasha shook her head. "You don't understand, do you?" she said.

"No," said Marc angrily. "It is YOU who do not understand. You are one of the Chosen Ones who live in comfort. I work deep in the mines every day. You are never hungry or cold. Look at your rich clothes ... and then look at what I wear."

He pulled aside his cloak. His old jerkin was dirty, and torn in many places.

"All this talk is a waste of breath," Sasha snapped back. "We do not have time to fight. We must go to the Radio Control Station at once."

"I agree," said Marc. He made to push past her. "We will argue about this no longer. I am going to the Prison."

Sasha moved quickly to block his way. She stood directly in front of Marc and folded her arms.

"Listen to me," she said. "You have the message capsule. It MUST be sent out tonight. If you go to the Prison you too may be taken. Think carefully. What would Con have wanted you to do?"

Chapter 6
A Disagreement

"He would want me to help him escape," Marc replied at once. "He would want to be free."

"That is not what I asked you," said Sasha. "I, too, would like to be free."

Marc laughed. "You *are* free. You live in the Fortress."

"Yes," said Sasha. "I live in the Fortress. But I am not free. Here, everyone is afraid. There are spies all around us. We cannot say what we choose, we cannot go where we please. No one is to be trusted. The films we see and the books we read have all been chosen for us. I do not call that freedom."

Marc was astonished. "You would rather live on the Outside where nothing is allowed to grow?"

"Sometimes I think I would," said Sasha. "They say that it was beautiful a long time ago, before the Keepers destroyed all the trees and grass."

"I have heard that too," said Marc.

"Well, it could be that way again," said Sasha. "If the Outsiders and the people in the Fortress work together."

"But first we must get rid of the Keepers," said Marc.

"Exactly," said Sasha.

Chapter 7
Jared the Keeper

Marc nodded his head slowly. Sasha took his arm.

"This way," she said.

Marc kept his hood up as he followed Sasha through the Fortress. She walked quickly, keeping to side streets and back alleys. No one challenged them. It was growing dark. Everyone was hurrying to be inside before curfew. Finally they came to a large building set back from the road.

"This is the Radio Control Station," said Sasha. "We must not go in together. The barrier gate will open when you place this card in the slot."

She handed Marc a thin square of plastic.

"Where did you get this?" asked Marc.

Sasha smiled. "There are others in the Fortress who think as I do. When inside, we will go to the basement. There, we can crawl along the air shafts to reach the transmission room. That's where they send out the electronic messages."

Ten minutes later Marc was almost glad of the time he had spent in the Merkonium mines. The air shafts were filthy and full of awkward twists. Ahead of him Sasha crawled fast, as agile as a cat. Eventually she stopped beside a metal grid.

She squinted through the slats.

"Here," she said softly. "My spies say that just after curfew the operator has a break for ten minutes or so. We will wait."

It was worse than hiding in the scrub bushes all day, thought Marc. There, he had been able to move a little to stretch his legs. Now they crouched in the half dark. They did not dare to move. They listened and waited.

Sasha touched him lightly. "He has gone out of the room," she said. She took a screwdriver from under her cloak and together they loosened the panel. Then they climbed down into the room. "The transmitter is just there."

Sasha pointed to a raised platform at one side of the room.

"Let us do it," said Marc.

He pulled the message capsule from his jerkin.

Sasha took the capsule from him.

"So small, yet so important," he said.

From outside the door Marc heard a noise. He grabbed Sasha's arm.

"Listen," he said.

There were footsteps in the corridor.

"Someone is coming," said Marc.

Sasha stretched up. She glanced through the glass panel at the top of the door.

She turned around to face Marc. Her whole body shook.

"We are lost," she whispered. "We are lost. It is Jared, the Keeper."

She shrank down in fear behind the door as it was flung open. A tall man stood in the doorway.

"Good evening, Marc," he said. "We meet again."

"Con!" Marc shouted out. He rushed forward. "You are free! How did you escape?"

Marc suddenly realised Con was not smiling. His face looked grim.

"It was very easy to escape," said Con. "I have my own key. The Prison belongs to me."

"What do you mean?" asked Marc.

And then the full meaning of what Sasha had just said entered Marc's brain.

When she had looked out into the corridor she had said, "We are lost ... It is Jared ..."

The man in front of Marc made a mock bow.

"Let me introduce myself to you properly, . boy," he said. "I am Con ... to you. But ... I am also Jared the Keeper."

Chapter 8
Betrayed

Marc staggered backwards.

"Is this a trick?" he gasped.

"Yes," said Jared. "And I'm sure that you will agree it is a very good one. Let me explain it to you, boy." He leaned closer to Marc. "The Outsider rebels know that a Starship from Earth comes close to our planet every twenty years. And ..." Jared paused and spoke very slowly,

"... we, the Keepers, *know* that they know this. Every twenty years we *expect* the Outsiders to revolt. We take it for granted that they will try to send an SOS to the visiting Starship."

Jared sneered at Marc. "So this time, I didn't wait for their usual hopeless attempt to get a message out. I decided to set it up myself. That way I would know *exactly* what you were all up to."

"You have betrayed us!" cried Marc.

"Yes, I suppose you might say that," said Jared. "But I think that I have done you all a favour. In past times, lots of lives were lost when the Outsiders attacked the Fortress. This plan has stopped that happening."

Marc was in despair.

"Why did you let me get this far?" he sobbed.

"You were not meant to get anywhere near the Radio Control Station," said Jared. "You should have been picked up at the gate, or in the Main Square. As time went on, and no one seemed to have seen you, I thought I'd better check here just in case."

"Why did you not wait to meet me in the Main Square?" said Marc. "Why did you make it seem that Con had been captured?"

"I did not want my cover broken. People would have seen me with you in the Square. Many in the Fortress know what Jared looks like. I want to be able to go back to the Outsiders as Con. I will report that, sadly, the plan failed. And then," Jared gave a horrible smile, "I will help them make a new plan for the next time."

"You will not always win," said Marc bravely. "Next time someone smarter will take my place."

"Don't be too hard on yourself, boy," said Jared. "You did very well to get this far. I believed that you would go to the Main Square, or, if you heard Con was captured, you would head straight for the Prison."

"I nearly did," said Marc. "But ..."

He stopped speaking. Sasha! It had been Sasha who had stopped him trying to rescue Con. It was she who had helped him get here. Where was she? What was she doing?

Jared had started to speak again. "I will deal with you, and then I must find out who this spy Alex is. But first, give me the message capsule."

"That too is a fake, I suppose," said Marc.

"No," said Jared. "You Outsiders have some knowledge of electronics. You would have known at once if the message was not a true one. The message capsule itself is real."

Marc drew in his breath. Sasha had the message capsule! And Jared had not seen her. Marc's heart began to race. Jared did not know the identity of the spy called Alex. He did not know about Sasha! They still had a chance!

"Hand over the message signal," said Jared.

"What?" said Marc.

As he spoke, Marc risked a quick glance beyond Jared's head. Behind Jared's back, Sasha was creeping inch by inch along the wall to the transmitter. She had the capsule in her hand. She was going to try to send the message! Marc realised he had to gain her a few more seconds.

Marc looked back to Jared. "But ... but I still don't understand," he stammered.

"There is nothing more for you to understand, boy," snapped Jared. "Give me the message capsule."

"No," said Marc.

"This is stupid," said Jared. "There is nothing to be gained by keeping it." He pulled his phaser from his belt. "Hand it over."

"I'd rather die," said Marc.

"Then die you will," said Jared, and he
raised his arm.

Chapter 9
Starship Rescue

"You will die with me," said Marc quickly.

Jared hesitated.

"What do you mean?" he said.

"You cannot fire a phaser in here," said Marc. "This room is not big enough."

Jared frowned, and then he shook his head.

"You are wrong," he said.

Marc was frantic. He must hold Jared's attention. He had to keep him talking.

He spoke fast. "In such a small space the build-up of energy would be huge. You would be caught in the blast."

"No, that is not correct," said Jared. There was a puzzled look on his face. "And you, boy, are smart enough to know that firing the phaser would not cause an explosion." He stared at Marc for a moment. "You are only playing for time. Why?"

Marc stared back.

Jared's eyes narrowed.

"Why?" he asked again. "Why are you trying to delay me?"

Marc said nothing.

Jared stepped across the room, and with a quick movement he grabbed Marc's shoulder.

"Give me the message capsule. Now!"

Marc tried to break free, but Jared's grip was firm. As they struggled Marc saw Sasha take her chance. She raced to the transmitter platform.

But as Marc saw her ... so did Jared.

"Ah!" he yelled. "Now I see what is happening! There is another traitor here!"

He raised his phaser and took aim.

"Stand back from the transmitter!" he shouted at Sasha. "Stand back or I fire!"

Sasha turned. She had opened the sending slot at the front of the transmitter.

Marc watched. All she had to do now was to drop the capsule inside, close the slot and press the start button. It would only take about three seconds. But it was three seconds she did not have.

Her shoulders dropped. The hand holding the capsule fell to her side.

Jared smiled.

"A wise move," he said.

Marc's whole body went limp. It was over. Once again the Outsiders had lost. Jared released his grip on his shoulder, and Marc slumped to the floor.

And then Marc noticed Sasha's arm move. Suddenly he realised that she had been bluffing so that Jared would drop his guard. She was going to do it!

"Stupid girl," Marc heard Jared snarl.

Jared fired his phaser, but as he did so, Marc leaped up to knock it out of his hand.

Sasha screamed as she was hit. She clutched her arm. The capsule fell, rolling across the floor.

As Jared bent down to pick up his phaser Marc kicked it away. Jared went after it, and Marc ran to help Sasha. She had picked up the capsule.

"Never mind me," she sobbed. "Send out the message."

Marc grabbed the capsule from her and placed it in the sending slot.

"Press that button and I will destroy you," Jared towered above him.

Marc looked at him calmly.

"Too late," he said, and he pressed the button.

There was a terrible silence in the room. Jared's face was hard and angry.

"You are too late, Jared," Marc said again. "Even if you had fired the phaser the message would still have gone. We both know that it only takes a micro second to transmit."

Jared gave a twisted smile. "So in the end, you were smart enough, boy." He backed away from Sasha and Marc. "Now, I think I should leave here at once," he said.

"Please stay where you are," said a voice behind him.

Four officers wearing Starfleet Security uniform had appeared in the room.

One of them lifted the visor of her helmet.

"I am Captain Mary Rand, Head of Security on Starship 9. We have beamed down to answer a distress call. Who can explain what is happening here?" she demanded.

Marc looked around. Two of the team had moved to take Jared's phaser from him. The other officer was attending to the phaser burn on Sasha's arm.

"I can try," said Marc.

Chapter 10
Mission Over?

"I could get used to this," Marc told Sasha later.

She was resting in hospital while her phaser burn healed. Marc was sitting beside her bed eating an orange. On a table in front of him was a bowl holding apples, grapes and bananas. Every so often Marc stretched over, picked one up, and examined it.

"I've never seen so much fruit all together at one time," he said.

Sasha laughed.

"Can you stop talking about food for one minute and tell me what is happening in the Fortress?" she said.

"Starfleet Security have taken over," said Marc. "They are setting up a new Council to govern our planet. The Outsiders and the people in the Fortress will work together. The Keepers are under arrest."

"And where is Jared now?" said Sasha.

"He is being questioned on the Starship," said Marc. "There is talk of sending him back to Earth to stand trial."

Sasha leaned back on her pillows.

"So our work is done," she said.

Marc bit into an apple. He grinned at Sasha.

"I think it may have just begun," he said.

Other Barrington Stoke titles available:-

What's Going On, Gus? by Jill Atkins 1-902260-10-4

Bungee Hero by Julie Bertagna 1-902260-23-6

Hostage by Malorie Blackman 1-902260-12-0

Ghost for Sale by Terry Deary 1-902260-14-7

Sam, the Detective by Terrance Dicks 1-902260-19-8

Billy the Squid by Colin Dowland 1-902260-04-X

Kick Back by Vivian French 1-902260-02-3

The Gingerbread House by Adèle Geras 1-902260-03-1

Virtual Friend by Mary Hoffman 1-902260-00-7

The Genie by Mary Hooper 1-902260-20-1

Tod in Biker City by Anthony Masters 1-902260-15-5

Wartman by Michael Morpurgo 1-902260-05-8

Extra Time by Jenny Oldfield 1-902260-13-9

Screw Loose by Alison Prince 1-902260-01-5

Life Line by Rosie Rushton -902260-21-X

Problems with a Python by Jeremy Strong 1-902260-22-8

Lift Off by Hazel Townson 1-902260-11-2

If you would like more information about the **BARRINGTON STOKE CLUB**, please write to:- Barrington Stoke Club, 10 Belford Terrace, Edinburgh, EH4 3DQ or visit our website at:-
www.barringtonstoke.co.uk